WRITTEN AND ILLUSTRATED BY ROB LEE
CONTRIBUTIONS BY SEB AND SARA MARKHAM,
STEPHEN FARRELL AND SANDRA LEE

£5.50
UK only

FiREMAN SAM
ANNUAL 1999

Contents

RUNAWAY ROSA

Trevor Evans had found Bella's cat Rosa wandering lost around the country lanes near Newtown. He returned Rosa to Bella.

"Ah, my poor-a-little baby!" cried Bella as she cuddled Rosa. "She got lost again."

"If she didn't run away so often she wouldn't keep getting lost," muttered Trevor under his breath.

Sarah and James stroked Rosa who purred contentedly.

Meanwhile Fireman Sam was enjoying a mug of tea before leaving for the station. He was reading a book of all the latest inventions. Soon the twins arrived and told Sam about Rosa's latest escapade. Sam's eyes lit up as he pointed to his book. "There's an invention in here that would be ideal for Bella!" he exclaimed. "It's called an electronic tracking device."

Sarah and James looked at Sam blankly.

Sam decided to make one. He scuttled to his inventing shed and began fiddling with little bits of machinery. Soon Sam emerged triumphantly from his shed and showed the twins his invention. It was a little tag to fit under Rosa's collar.

"What does it do, Uncle Sam?" asked Sarah. Sam produced a little monitor. "Whenever Rosa runs away this little monitor will tell us at the station where she is so that we can keep track of her."

"It's brill!" cried James.

"Perhaps you should make one for Mrs Price so she can keep track of naughty Norman!" chuckled Sarah.

Next, Sam got a lift from Trevor Evans to the fire station. Sam explained to Trevor about his new invention and asked him if he would deliver Rosa's tag to Bella.

Later at the station Sam and Elvis were washing Jupiter.

It had been a quiet day so far with no call-outs.

"I'm getting peckish, Elvis," said Sam. "What's for lunch?"

"I've ordered a jumbo pepperoni pizza from Bella's cafe to be delivered to the station," replied Elvis.

"Yummee!" said Sam licking his lips.

"It'll be a while," said Elvis. "Would you like a bowl of my home-made turnip and cabbage stew while you wait?" Sam

gulped nervously at the thought. "...Er, no. I'll wait thanks, Elvis," he said. "It, er doesn't pay to have too much of a good thing."

Just then Station Officer Steele called from the station office. "Jump to it, men! Rosa's gone missing again!"

Sam and Elvis clambered aboard Jupiter and raced away from the station.

"No need to panic," said Sam confidently as he pulled the monitor from his pocket. He switched it on and it began bleeping merrily away.

"Bingo!" exclaimed Sam. "The tag under Rosa's collar is sending out a strong signal. We'll be able to follow her easily."

Elvis steered Jupiter through the country lanes as Sam read

directions from the monitor.

"Turn left at the next junction and head towards Pandy Lane, Elvis," commanded Sam.

Then he shouted, "Quickly, turn right at Newtown Crossroads and head towards Pontypandy..."

Soon Sam realised that he wasn't catching up with Rosa. "I can't understand it," he muttered. "According to this monitor Rosa must be travelling at about thirty miles an hour!"

Elvis kept following Sam's directions until suddenly he realised they were heading back to the fire station.

Meanwhile at the station, Trevor Evans was delivering the jumbo pepperoni pizza to

Station Officer Steele.

"My word, that smells tasty, Trevor," chuckled Steele.

Just then Sam and Elvis dashed into the mess room.

"Where's Rosa?" asked Sam.

"I haven't seen her," replied Steele.

"That's strange," said Sam. "According to my monitor Rosa's tag should be in the station."

Trevor suddenly looked embarrassed. "Good Lord!" he gulped, pulling the little electronic tag from his pocket. "I was so busy I forgot to deliver the tag to Bella."

Sam groaned, "Great fires of London! It wasn't Rosa we've been following all afternoon. It was Trevor's bus!"

"So that's why it was moving so fast," muttered Elvis.

"That means we still have to find Rosa," groaned Sam.

"But first let's have our pizza," said Steele, "I'm famished."

Later Sam and Elvis went

searching for Rosa. They decided to call at Bella's cafe to see if Rosa had returned home.

"I haven't-a-seen her," said Bella sadly, "she's-a-been gone for hours!"

"Don't get yourself in a state, Bella," said Sam gently. "She'll turn up sooner or later."

Just then Elvis pricked up an ear. "Ssh!" he exclaimed.

In the silence they all heard the faint sound of purring. Sam followed the sound to the cafe storeroom. He quietly opened the door to find Rosa happily snoozing away amongst the boxes.

"Good grief!" chuckled Sam. "She was here all the time!"

"Cara mia!" cried Bella. "I must have-a-locked poor Rosa in when I went to the cafe storeroom for the pepperoni for your pizza."

"At least she didn't go hungry," laughed Elvis as Rosa stirred herself.

Sam handed the tag over to Bella and said, "In future you'll never have to worry about losing her."

Just then Rosa scampered across the cafe before Bella could put the tag on her and disappeared through the cat flap into the street!

"I wouldn't bet on it!" groaned Elvis!

WORD SEARCH

HELP BELLA AND DILYS FIND ROSA'S NAME.
IT APPEARS SIX TIMES IN THE BOXES BELOW.

P	O	S	E	B	S	Q	L
O	E	A	R	X	L	O	E
S	O	R	O	S	A	V	A
A	P	V	S	X	E	R	M
R	O	S	A	T	M	O	O
Z	W	K	S	R	O	S	A
R	O	B	J	F	R	A	T
R	O	S	A	S	A	R	A

TROUBLE IN STORE!

SAM IS CHECKING HIS STORES. HE FINDS THAT THERE ARE TWO OF EVERYTHING EXCEPT FOR ONE ITEM. CAN YOU FIND THE ODD ITEM? SAM HAS NOTICED THAT THERE ARE MICE IN THE STORE. HOW MANY MICE ARE THERE?

COPY COLOUR!
TRY TO COPY COLOUR THIS PICTURE

SAM'S NEW INVENTION

Sam had been so busy lately he'd had no time to do any housework. His house was full up with crumpled clothes that needed ironing.

As Sam headed for work he couldn't help noticing his overgrown garden. "My goodness," groaned Sam. "My garden looks like a flipping jungle."

Meanwhile Norman was playing tricks on his mum. He photographed her surprise when his frog leapt out of the biscuit jar. Dilys screamed.

Norman had entered a competition for the funniest photo. "That was a good one," chuckled Norman as he scampered away from his very angry mum.

Later, Norman dropped sticky chewing gum on the pavement. Soon, Trevor Evans stepped in it. "Gotcha!" laughed Norman as he snapped away.

Next, it was Sarah's turn. Norman had swapped her fried egg for a rubber one. "This will make a really funny photo!" he giggled, to himself.

A little while later Norman spotted Fireman Sam taking a short cut through the woods on his way to work. Norman had an idea.

Norman asked Sam if he would pose for a photo. "I'd be delighted," said Sam. "Just step back a little bit, Sam," said Norman craftily.

"Just a little bit more," said Norman as Sam edged his way backwards and fell into the river! Sam spluttered angrily as he splashed about in the water.

"Say cheese!" called Norman as he snapped away at a very angry and soaked Sam. "You little monster!" gurgled Sam as he struggled to his feet.

Suddenly Sam felt something unusual on the river bed. "Great fires of London!" he cried. "I've found a necklace." "Cor!" muttered Norman.

Sam and Norman examined the necklace. "It looks valuable," said Sam. "I'd better take it to the police station to see if they can find the owner."

A few days later Sam received a letter from the station. The owner of the necklace had been found and in the envelope was a fifty pounds reward!

Sam scurried to the scrap yard and bought lots of bits of metal. "I'll invent something that will help me and Norman," smiled Sam, as he headed home.

Sam spent all day in his inventing shed tinkering with bits of metal. Then he called Norman to come and see. "Brill!" cried Norman, at the strange sight.

Before long Norman was snapping away at Sam's new invention. "I'm bound to win the competition now!" chuckled Norman excitedly. Sam beamed.

THIS IS THE AMAZING SIGHT THAT NORMAN WAS PHOTOGRAPHING. SAM HAD INVENTED TWO ROBOTS TO DO HIS WASHING, IRONING AND GARDENING. "SIX HANDS ARE BETTER THAN ONE!" CHUCKLED SAM.

SAM'S NEW INVENTION IS ABOUT TO DECORATE THE HOUSE!
CAN YOU UNSCRAMBLE THE LETTERS TO FIND OUT WHICH 4
COLOURS SAM HAS CHOSEN? THEN COLOUR THE PICTURE.

"ARE YOU RECEIVING ME...?"
HELP JAMES FIND A CLEAR LINE TO SARAH
THROUGH ALL THE STATIC INTERFERENCE!

THE PICTURE BELOW HAS BEEN JUMBLED UP. PASTE IT ON TO A PIECE OF CARD THEN CUT IT INTO SEGMENTS BY CUTTING ALONG THE BLACK LINES. NOW YOU HAVE YOUR OWN JIGSAW.

COLOURING FUN!

WHILE YOU ARE COLOURING THIS PICTURE, COUNT
HOW MANY EGGS NORMAN HAS GOT FOR EASTER.

SAM'S DECORATING DISASTER

Fireman Sam was on his way to the station when he bumped into Sarah and James. They were going fishing.

"Bella has promised to fry us fish and chips for tea if we catch a fish," said James. "Would you like to come to tea, Uncle Sam?"

"Just try to stop me," replied Sam, excitedly. "Make sure you catch a big one!"

Next, Sam bumped into Trevor Evans whose face was covered in ink.

"What happened to you?" chuckled Sam.

"That flippin' Norman Price squirted me with his trick fountain pen," grumbled Trevor.

"You'd better hope it's washable ink, Trev," smiled Sam as he waved goodbye.

Then Sam heard a loud scream coming from Dilys Price's shop. Seconds later Norman Price flew out of the shop and raced down the road followed by a saucepan which just missed him.

Sam went inside the shop where he saw Dilys covered in ink. Dilys was very angry.

"Look at my best lounge, Sam," she wailed.

Sam saw that the wallpaper was covered in ink splashes. He tried to console Dilys. "It's not too bad, Dil," he said. "We're painting the fire station today, if we finish early I'll pop back and help you clean up your lounge."

Later, at the station, Elvis poured Sam a mug of tea before

putting a joint of meat in the oven.

Elvis was grumbling about the dilapidated oven. "It's bloomin' ancient," he griped. "And I'm sure I can smell gas."

"That's probably one of Norman's stink bombs," said Sam. "He's been playing pranks all morning."

Just then Steele arrived with his duty rota. He explained to the crew that the station needed a facelift inside and out. Steele led the men to the store room where he issued the paint, brushes and ladders.

"Let's hope we get a quiet day," said Sam later, as he and Elvis began preparing to paint Steele's office. Just as he spoke Steele called the men to the mess.

"Quickly crew!" shouted Steele. "Trevor Evans is trapped on his roof!"

Sam and the crew were soon speeding through Pontypandy, sirens blaring, lights flashing. They arrived at Trevor's and quickly unloaded the ladders.

"Help!" wailed Trevor as he clung on to the television aerial.

"Don't worry, Trev," said Sam as he clambered up the ladder. "You're safe now."

Sam helped Trevor down the ladder to safety. Trevor thanked Sam and explained that he was trying to adjust the aerial to get a better picture on his T.V.

"What were you watching?" asked Elvis.

"A programme about mountaineering," replied Trevor.

"In that case you should have

known how to get down!" chuckled Sam. The crew laughed loudly.

Meanwhile Sarah and James had caught a fish in Pandy River but as James tried to net it he fell in! Sarah couldn't reach James so she ran to the nearest phone and called Sam. Sam and the crew were on the way back to the station when they received the call. Sam spun Jupiter around and raced to the river.

When they arrived Steele spotted James clinging to a rock in the river.

"We won't reach him from the bank," said Steele. "One of us will have to go in!"

"I'll go, sir," said Sam.

Before long Sam had waded across the river and grabbed a relieved James.

Safely back on the bank, Sam pointed to the net which contained a large fish. He chuckled, "At least you didn't lose the fish, James. Well done."

Sam gave Sarah and James a lift back to Pontypandy. As he drove off Bella appeared. She was delighted at the size of the fish the twins had caught.

"Ah, fresh fish and chips," exclaimed Bella. "Ees bellissimo!"

As the crew drove towards the station, Sam hoped that the rest of the day would be quiet so that they could get on with the painting. Suddenly the phone in the cab rang. Steele answered then called to the men. "About turn. There's a fire at Pontypandy Gasworks!"

Jupiter sped past a bewildered Bella and the twins, its siren blaring.

"Caramia!" exclaimed Bella.

Minutes later Sam called to Steele to give him accurate directions to the Gasworks. Steele and Elvis looked back at Sam blankly. Sam slammed on the brakes and Jupiter screeched to a halt.

"Hang on!" muttered Sam. "There's no Gasworks in Pontypandy. We've been had!"

"Someone's playing a prank," sighed Steele. "Probably naughty flippin' Norman Price!"

Meanwhile back at the station, Norman Price was loitering around looking for more

mischief to get into. Suddenly his nose twitched. "Cor! I can smell a stink bomb...'ang on...that's gas!"

Next thing Elvis's cooker, which had a slow gas leak after all, blew up with a mighty BANG!

"Wow!" cried Norman as the windows blew out of the station. He rushed to the phone and called Sam and the crew to raise the alarm.

In the cab Steele answered the phone. He listened then replied, "Oh yes? Next you'll be telling me the moon is made of green cheese!" Steele replaced the receiver with a thump and told the crew that Norman had phoned to say that the station was on fire.

"That boy's a little pest!" said Sam grimly.

Just then Elvis noticed a plume of smoke coming from

the station. "Look!" he cried.

"Great fires of London!" exclaimed Sam as he put his foot down and sped Jupiter towards the station.

Sam and the crew raced into action.

They jumped down and

manned the hoses. Steele directed their aim. Soon they had the blaze under control.

As the final embers flickered out Steele surveyed the scene.

Sam mopped his brow and looked around the mess. "It could have been worse," he said. "It could have happened after we'd decorated instead of before!"

"You're right, Sam," said Steele chirpily. "We'll soon have this place shipshape."

"And I'll soon have a new oven," chuckled Elvis. "Brill!"

"It probably won't improve the cooking," said Sam under his breath.

"Ang on," said Elvis. "Until I get my new cooker we'll have to have sandwiches and things."

Steele looked quite relieved at missing Elvis's cooking. Sam wasn't so happy as he was famished. His eyes suddenly lit up as he remembered he'd been invited to Bella's for fish and chips. "Yummee!" said Sam happily.

The next day Sam and the crew worked very hard and soon the station was painted. It looked a treat. Sam noticed that there were a few pots of paint left over. He scratched his chin thoughtfully.

Later, Sam drove to Dilys Price's shop. Norman and Dilys were behind the counter. Sam explained to Dilys about the trouble Norman had caused with his false alarm.

"It's a very naughty thing to do," said Sam to the shame faced Norman. "It means we're busy on a wild goose chase while there could be a really serious accident happening."

Dilys was about to send Norman to his room when Sam interrupted. He whispered to Dilys who chuckled.

Later Sam waved Dilys goodbye as she stood watch over Norman as he painted his mum's lounge for her using Sam's left over paint.

"That'll keep him too busy to cause any mischief today," smiled Sam as he climbed aboard Jupiter. He was about to drive off when he smelled something ghastly. Then he realised he'd sat on one of Norman's carefully placed stink bombs!

"Norman flippin' Price!" groaned Sam.

BE A COPYCAT!

DREAM PUZZLE

CAN YOU COMPLETE THIS CROSSWORD? THE ITEMS BELOW THE MAIN PICTURE ARE YOUR CLUES.

MAD SCRAMBLE!

SAM HAS TO DELIVER FIRE EXTINGUISHERS TO LOTS OF PEOPLE ON HIS LIST. THE NAMES HAVE GOT JUMBLED UP IN HIS TELEX MACHINE. CAN YOU HELP HIM UNSCRAMBLE THEM?

ANSWER: BELLA, NORMAN, TREVOR, PENNY.

34

TWINS TEASER!

CAREFULLY TRY TO COPY THE PICTURE OF THE PUPPY INTO THE EMPTY GRID BELOW.

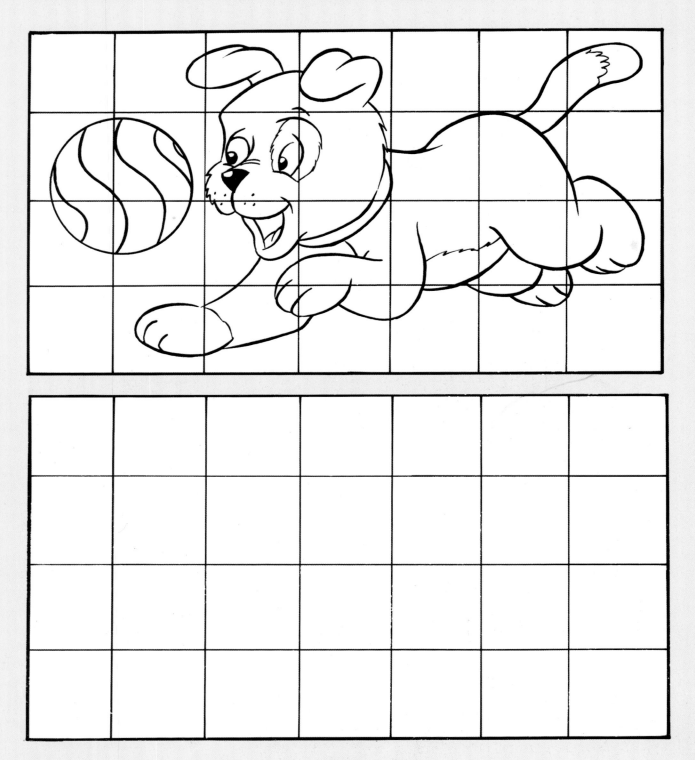

MAKE A JIGSAW!

HERE'S A JIGSAW FOR YOU TO MAKE!
ASK AN ADULT TO HELP YOU PASTE IT ONTO A PIECE
OF CARD AND CUT OUT ALL THE PIECES. NOW SEE IF
YOU CAN PUT IT BACK TOGETHER!

ODD ONE OUT!

CAN YOU SPOT WHICH SOCK IS THE ODD ONE OUT?

THE LOST KITE!

Fireman Sam called in to see Sarah and James. He'd brought them a kite. "You'll have to share it," said Sam. "But remember, no fighting!"

It was a lovely windy day so Sarah and James went out to the countryside to fly the kite. "You've had it ages," moaned James grumpily.

They both tugged at the kite. "It's my turn!" cried James. Next they lost their grip on the kite and it flew high into the sky.

Soon it had flown out of sight. The twins found Sam in the cafe and explained. Sam said he would keep an eye out for the kite.

Later that day Penny was driving back to Newtown Station when she spotted the twins' kite. "Goodness, it's miles away," she said.

Trevor was on his allotment when the kite flew by. "Daro! The twins' kite is flying away from Pontypandy!" he groaned.

Norman and his mum Dilys were next to see the kite. It was such a windy day the kite flew out of sight in no time. Dilys sighed.

"I'm afraid you'll never get your kite back now!" said Dilys to the twins later. "It must be halfway to Cardiff by now!"

Just then Sam arrived with a lovely brand new kite for the twins. "I had to drive to Cardiff to buy this little beauty!" he chuckled.

The twins were delighted but soon started squabbling about who should have first go. Suddenly Sam heard a flapping noise from above.

"Great fires of London!" he cried as he saw the kite. "It must have got tangled onto Jupiter when I drove back from Cardiff!" he chuckled.

"Now we can have a kite each!" said Sarah. "There'll be no need to argue." "I'll believe that when I see it!" laughed Sam.

BELLA, NORMAN, SAM AND SARAH ARE EACH HOLDING A KITE. CAN YOU SEE WHICH KITE BELONGS TO WHICH CHARACTER, AND WHICH ONE IS SPARE?

SAM AND THE TWINS ARE PLAYING IN THE COUNTRYSIDE. CAN YOU FIND FOUR ITEMS IN THE BOXES THAT DON'T APPEAR IN THE MAIN PICTURE?

LEARN TO DRAW!

HAVE FUN WHILE YOU LEARN TO DRAW BY FINISHING OFF THE PICTURES BELOW.

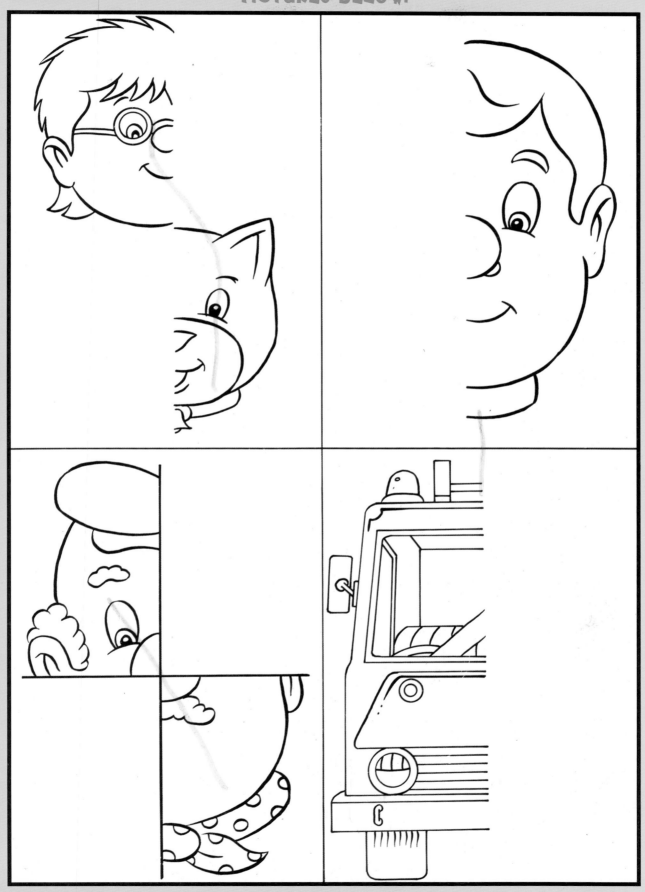

43

SAM'S FULL HOUSE!

CUT OUT AND PASTE THE PICTURES AROUND SAM'S HOUSE, THEN CAREFULLY PLACE THEM IN THEIR CORRECT SPACES.

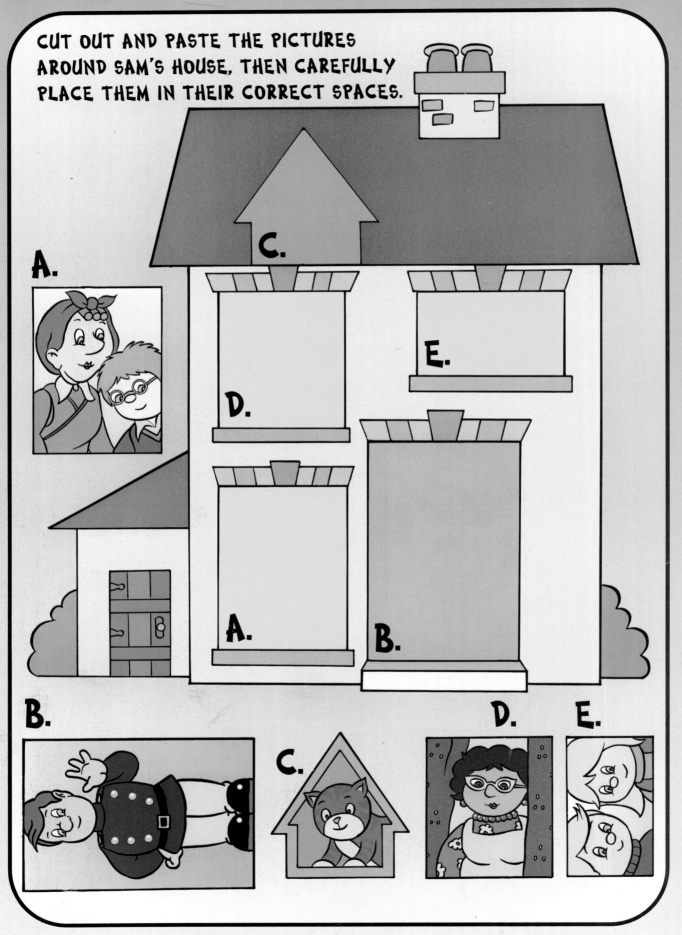

SOMETHING TO CHEW ON!

SAM HAS ASKED BELLA TO COOK HIS FAVOURITE BREAKFAST. IF YOU TAKE THE INITIALS OF THE ITEMS IN THE BOX BELOW AND RE-ARRANGE THEM YOU WILL FIND OUT WHAT SAM HAS ORDERED.

PICTURE POSER!

THERE ARE FIVE PICTURES OF BELLA AND TREVOR. ONLY TWO ARE IDENTICAL. CAN YOU SPOT THEM?

JUMBLED UP PICS

SAM AND THE CREW WERE PRACTISING FIRST AID BUT IT ALL WENT WRONG. SOON THEY HAD A REAL ACCIDENT TO DEAL WITH. THE ARTIST ALSO GOT THE PICTURES JUMBLED UP. SEE IF YOU CAN PUT THEM IN THE RIGHT ORDER.

A

B

C

D

E

PICNIC PUZZLE!
WHICH PATH DO THE TWINS TAKE TO GET TO BELLA'S PICNIC?

COLOURING FUN!

CAT-ASTROPHE!

It was Norman's bath day but he hated baths. He preferred playing with his cap gun. He couldn't resist firing it before dashing out of the house.

Norman wandered all over Pontypandy firing his gun. "The Cactus Kid is in town!" he hollered. The sound of his gun frightened poor Rosa the cat.

Rosa dashed off in fright. James didn't see her coming and lost control of his skateboard. "Whoaa!" he cried as he almost fell off.

Unable to stop himself James sped into the road. Just then Sam was driving by and had to swerve to avoid James. "Look out!" he cried.

As Sam swerved to avoid James, Jupiter skidded towards the grass verge. Bella was nearby and leapt out of the fire engine's path. "Cara mia!" she cried.

Sam stopped Jupiter and stepped out of the cab. "Are you alright?" he asked Bella. "I-a-will-be when I'm out of this ditch!" she wailed.

He helped Bella out to safety then went looking for culprit Norman Price! "Here he is!" muttered Sam as he dashed after Norman. Norman raced off.

Sam chased Norman all over Pontypandy until Norman tripped over a kerb and flew into the air before landing in a smelly dustbin!

Norman had fallen into the chip shop's dustbin. He smelt so strongly of fish that all the cats in town began chasing him. "Oh, no!" he wailed as he dashed off.

The very smelly Norman ran for miles before shaking off the cats. "I'm exhausted," puffed Norman. He decided to head home for tea and a lie down.

When he arrived home his mum had other ideas. "It's in the bath for you my boy!" she said firmly. "And early to bed for causing so much trouble today!"

Dilys threw Norman's noisy gun away. Sam arrived later with a new one. Norman's eyes lit up until he fired it. "That's much better!" laughed Sam and Dilys.

DOT-TO-DOT!

SAM IS WISHING FOR SOMETHING NICE TO GIVE THE TWINS.
JOIN THE DOTS TO SEE WHAT IT IS.

GOING AROUND IN CIRCLES!

HERE'S A GAME YOU CAN PLAY WITH YOUR PALS. THROW A SIX TO START AND FOLLOW THE INSTRUCTIONS IN THE BOXES. TRY TO HELP SAM FIND ROSA. WHAT SAM DOESN'T REALISE IS THAT ROSA WAS ON JUPITER ALL THE TIME!

START

1

SEARCH PONTYPANDY MINESHAFT. MISS A GO

FINISH

YOU FIND ROSA ON JUPITER!

10.

9.

8.

GET A FLAT TYRE. STOP TO CHANGE WHEEL. MISS A GO

J 999

PICNIC PUZZLE

THE FOUR SMALL PICTURES ARE TAKEN FROM THE BIG PICTURE. CAN YOU SEE WHERE THEY BELONG?

ROSA'S POSER

ROSA LOVES CREAM CAKE. CAN YOU HELP HER
REACH IT WITHOUT BUMPING INTO BELLA?

NORMAN'S SNAPSHOTS
WHICH ONE THESE PHOTOS DIDN'T NORMAN TAKE?

COPY COLOUR!

SAM AND THE TWINS ARE PLAYING SNOWBALLS. LOOK CAREFULLY AT THE COLOURS IN THE PICTURE ABOVE AND TRY TO COPY THEM IN THE PICTURE BELOW.